Salvage
Short and Shorter Stories

KEVIN HUGHES

ISBN: 979-8-218-18419-3

For my wife, Mary Carol, who continues to grow a garden
in my heart

For my son, Josh, whose optimism and enthusiasm for
life continue to inspire me

None of them knew the color of the sky.

— Stephen Crane, "The Open Boat"

ACKNOWLEDGMENTS

My heartfelt thanks to my long-time friend and story editor, Mary Simmons, who inspired me to complete this project, which began some years ago. She recommended transitional text, addressed continuity, and suggested elaboration where needed.

Much gratitude to my friend and copy editor, Lorien Megill, for giving my stories the polish they needed before going to press. I enjoy her sense of humor almost as much as her astute attention to grammar, punctuation, and clarity of expression.

Thanks to my buddy and incomparable graphic designer, Mario Ruiz, for converting the themes of my stories into this wonderful book cover. Mario has designed print media, interactive courseware, CD artwork, and music videos for me throughout my career.

With love to my wife, Mary Carol—my confidant, my motivator, and one who is as committed to artistic expression as I am.

CONTENTS

PREFACE

Thank you for opening my book. The four short stories that begin this book started out either as oral stories told to friends or as written histories of semi-personal experiences I felt ought to be recorded. As an avid reader of fiction, I suppose I have always been attentive to interesting people I meet, events that happen to me or around me, and snippets of observations that alter my view of the world.

The second part of this book is dedicated to even smaller pieces of life that I have titled Shorter Stories. These eschew the beginning, middle, and end of a traditional tale by capturing single events that struck me as enchanting, humorous, or deeply moving. These range from fanciful childhood memories of inverting the world and walking on the ceiling to remembering a friend and journalist who was tripped up by an inquisitive public-school student following his stirring presentation on career day.

Which brings me to why I composed the stories in this—my first book. I was a deliriously happy English major hoping to find a career where I could read the great novels and discuss them over coffee with other English majors. Somehow this impractical decision eventually led to my first job as a technical writer, which in turn flowed into proposal writing, then instructional design for web users, and finally to producing and directing videos for a major corporation. Oh yes, and I am also a lifelong musician and songwriter.

My greatest hope is that you will lose yourself in these stories, ponder them—or dismiss them—laugh with them, or recognize the value of learning just a little bit more about people, places, and things.

SALVAGE

Dad guided the giant Oldsmobile up the steady incline of Route 66, past the Short Stop Diner and the old deserted motel, toward the crest of Nine-Mile Hill.

I always loved the sound of Nine-Mile Hill. As a kid fed on fifties television, the name conjured up images of cowboy Roy Rogers riding Trigger at a full gallop to the top of the mesa where a stage holdup is in progress. He'd shoot the guns out of the outlaws' hands, tie them up, and herd them back to town for an appointment with the sheriff.

"I think it's nine miles from the center of downtown to the top of the mesa," said Dad, flicking the ash of his Camel cigarette into the ashtray below the dashboard.

Dad looked so cool in his Hawaiian shirt, with his wrist draped lazily over the top of the steering wheel. He hadn't put on too much weight back then, and his jet-black hair, muscular arms, and copper skin still caught people's attention. It's funny, looking back—there we were, cruising up the two-lane highway at sixty miles an hour, relaxed in the front seat without any seat belts—and I felt safer than I ever have since.

The salvage yard was just about the last sign of human habitation on the way out of town. Only one place out-reached it: the 66 Drive-In theater, which supposedly featured pretty "raunchy" movies. This was Dad's way of telling me that they weren't fit for kids.

Dad maneuvered the Olds into the lot and parked over an oily patch of dirt in front of two green 55-gallon drums filled with discarded engine parts. He grabbed the carbure-tor wrapped in an old hand towel and the small toolbox off the back seat, and swung the door closed with a loud clunk. I followed him into the dilapidated front office.

The salvage and auto repair shop was a magical place. It smelled of an odd combination of tire rubber, gasoline, sol-vents, dust, and cigarette smoke. Beneath the windows on three sides of the office, thick wooden counters extended from the walls, with table legs to support them every six feet or so. The counters housed well-used telephone direc-tories, dozens of parts catalogues and inventory records, assorted engine parts, grease rags, and an occasional empty soda-pop bottle. Horseflies buzzed and thumped against the windows, tirelessly looking for an exit before their lives ran out.

And then there were the calendars: one with tractors and farm equipment, another with aerial shots of a New England village with the obligatory white church steeple jutting through the red and orange foliage. The "True Ser-vice" calendar displayed colored-pencil illustrations of young women sprawled over the hoods of huge automobiles. Dad never seemed to notice them, but I found them oddly stimulating without knowing exactly why.

I loved watching Dad interact with the salvage men. These were guys who grew up working on automobiles, and machinery was their religion. The chain of events that begins with a spark, igniting the mixture of air and gasoline, forcing rods to turn a crankshaft that turns the wheels, that propel the car forward—this was the only truth they knew. Now they helped weekend mechanics like my Dad replace old worn-out parts with less worn-out parts. They were a little like grave robbers whose cadavers and body parts could be obtained for the right price. From these parts, our fathers and brothers—and probably a sister or two—spent hours trying to reanimate the family automobiles.

It was fun to watch one of the men regard my father—with arms folded across his chest, eyes squinting from the smoke of a cigarette—listening to Dad's description of what he needed. Sometimes their expressions showed acknowledgment, other times subtle condescension, but to me, Dad's knowledge of cars was indisputable. I figured that was why they always addressed him as "Mr. Davis." It never occurred to me that they addressed all their customers this way.

On this particular visit, Dad fiddled with the throttle plate on an old carburetor while one of the salvage men paged through a list of automobile wrecks in the yard. Behind us, two men in overalls talked loudly about the baseball season. The taller man took pulls on a Grape Nehi soda, while the other ate what looked like a ham sandwich on white bread. He held the sandwich delicately with both hands—kind of how you might cradle a harmonica. Both hands were covered with brownish-black smudges, all the way to his wrists.

"Bingo," said the man with "Henry" stitched on his work shirt. He'd found a match for Dad's part. He tore a piece of paper off an old invoice and jotted down the lot and space number where the car would be found. With a slow and deliberate manner, he led us out into the shimmering maze of wrecked automobiles.

The sight of hundreds of cars of every make and model and in varying degrees of decrepitude was exhilarating. Some teetered over the ground, supported by cinder blocks or railroad ties. Others lay inert in the dry dust. For every car that exposed a skeleton stripped of doors and fenders and hoods, there was another so crunched and mangled you'd be hard pressed to salvage a door handle or trunk latch. Front windshields, if intact at all, displayed spiderweb shatter points where flying metal—or people—had collided with them. A few cars lay inverted with their chassis facing skyward.

In those days, my favorite cars were the heavy Detroit jobs—the late-1950s Thunderbirds, Chevy Bel Airs, and Buicks. I got a kick out of the round headlight eyes sometimes recessed beneath a hooded brow, the grill full of teeth, and the occasional Art Deco hood ornament.

Dad liked the older cars—the classics—as he called them, with their big rounded fenders, running boards, and small oval rear windshields. The same vintage automobiles Hollywood gangsters drove in those black-and-white movies we used to watch on our old Zenith.

The three of us tromped through the windblown sand past dozens of automobiles before Henry brought us to Dad's treasure—a 1955 Ford Fairlane. He forced open the hood and, raising it with a loud creak, exposed the engine.

The salvage man left us in the glare of the metallic

graveyard to extract our engine part. Dad compared his carburetor with the one in the Fairlane to be sure it matched.

"Son, you want to see how this thing comes out?" he said, resting his elbow on my shoulder.

"Sure."

Using a rusted wheel as a riser, I leaned over the front fender to watch Dad work. But it wasn't long before my fidgeting caused him to ask if I wouldn't rather go play in one of the old cars while he finished up. Dad and I both knew it was against the yard's policy to let anyone play in or around the cars, but we'd never been reprimanded. As I took off into a full run, I heard him call after me:

"And watch out for spiders. For heaven's sake, don't get bit by a black widow."

I chose a huge water tanker with an exposed cab so high off the ground I had to pull myself up using the door frame. My high-top tennis shoes clopped loudly as I tumbled down onto the tattered seat. The coils in the seat were so worn that I bounced a couple of times, like I'd seen truck drivers do when they came to an abrupt stop.

I can still smell the decayed fabric and rusted metal and oily dust. The history of this machine lurked somewhere in that odor—who drove it, which roads it traveled, who kept it running faithfully, why it ended its life in this automotive boneyard.

I pretended to drive the giant water tanker, trying to turn the steering wheel an inch or two in either direction. I yanked back and forth on the gearshift protruding through a hole in the cab's floor. All the while, I kept an eye out for the salvage man or for Dad coming to fetch me.

Eventually, I jumped from the cab, landing ungracefully onto a wisp of fine sand. I returned to Dad's spot as he was closing up his small toolbox.

"Okay, Tiger, let's head back," he said. "Mom'll be lookin' for us."

As we walked back to our car, Dad stopped abruptly and let out a sigh.

"Look at those mountains, will ya?" He motioned toward the mile-high Sandias that border Albuquerque on the east. They stood a pale blue-gray against the azure sky.

"Aren't they somethin'?" he added.

"They look flat like a piece of cardboard," I said.

"That's because of the sunlight. 'Bout seven o'clock tonight the sun'll be throwing long shadows back into those canyons." This was Dad just enjoying the moment, like he did back then. We'd be sitting in the living room watching a movie on TV, and he'd up and say, "That Steve McQueen—what a natural actor!" or, "Boy, they walked into it this time! Don't know how they're gonna get out of this one." Then he'd laugh out loud and slap his hand on the arm of the old easy chair.

In those days, Dad took pleasure in so many things: taking the family to drive-in movies, playing golf with his buddies from the Lab, taking me to the airport to watch the planes take off and land, working in the yard with his shirt off, chatting over the fence with our eccentric next-door neighbor, watching Mickey Mantle hit one into the stands. And rummaging around salvage yards with me.

Just short of my teen years, Dad and I did other things together that I like to remember. We played catch—although he chased my bad throws more than caught them. We built model airplanes and hung them from the ceiling in my room. I lit the charcoal in the barbeque grill for him on holidays and offered to help him work on the car whenever he was making his own repairs. It was then that we both discovered auto mechanics was not "my thing," though I did learn how a carburetor and an internal combustion engine work.

Then high school came, and I began to drift away from him. He was mystified by my disinterest in sports and grew concerned whenever he'd find me conducting an imaginary orchestra to the phonograph in my bedroom. Just outside the door, I can still hear him saying to Mom, "I'm worried about that boy."

Speaking of Mom, she was the "human" mechanic in our home. It was she who was getting us off to school and driving me and my brother Cliff to Cub Scout meetings and birthday parties. And it was Mom who always asked those "kid maintenance" questions:

"Does it hurt when I press here?"

"Do you feel like you need to throw up?"

"When was this homework due?"

She cooked for us, nursed us back to health, and generally fretted over us. But Dad, the 1960s patriarch, slowly faded out of the picture.

I think my going to college was the defining moment in our eroding relationship. I evolved into the quintessential collegian: I knew everything there was to know; I railed about middle class values and consumerism—the evil that was born when my Dad went to college on the G.I. Bill; got a good job at the Labs; and paid for my college education, my electric guitar, and our upright piano. Of course, I saw no hypocrisy in my perspective. In my mind, the professors and text books had it "right."

The worst of our conflicts came when Dad asked me what I was going to do with a degree in music, English, or film.

After voicing a litany of obscure reasons for my degree choices, I declared, "I just want to be happy, Dad."

"Happy! Who's happy?!" he shot back. "You go to

school, you get a job, you have a family, and you take care of them! Who has time to be happy?"

Years later I came to the realization that separating from my parent's influence was healthy, and when I moved away, things got marginally better. Still, I saw that while my confidence grew, so too did Dad's disillusionment. As the arc of my trajectory widened, his fell to earth—weighted I suppose by his resignation to an unfinished life. I should have been more sensitive to it. Even with all his career honors and awards lovingly placed on the walls of the family room, Dad sometimes looked as though he were trying to remember something.

Then, our family was rocked by an unexpected event. Cliff began to exhibit behavior linked to mental illness, which slowly masked a brilliant intellect. While this changed our whole family dynamic, Dad took it the hardest. His reaction began with denial and turned quickly to anger. I think he must have seen this as his own failure. It's not like there were any support groups back then. In the middle-class world, your confidant was usually a golf pro, bartender, or minister. Just saying "mental illness" out loud in conversation was like vomiting in public.

Maybe because of Cliff, I pushed myself relentlessly to earn my college degree and maintain a high grade-point average. I spent long hours in the Fine Arts department's catacombs practicing Bach and Beethoven piano pieces without any sense of what I could do with a degree in music. A semester or two later, an art professor convinced me I could be a courtroom artist, and contacted two public defenders who recommended that I attend public trials to produce sample sketches of judges, attorneys, and defendants. A spark never caught with this pursuit either. After fumbling through another semester, I finally hit on film theory and history, which became a springboard for my career as a producer and director of corporate videos.

When I graduated, I could see the disappointment in Dad's eyes. He realized that I'd never manage a university athletic department or earn a scholarship to an Ivy League School of Business and Finance. I'd never deliver my closing arguments in a courtroom or prescribe medication to an ailing patient. I was simply his youngest son—the one with a liberal education who only "wanted to be happy."

* * *

Many years later, after Dad got sick, I was startled by the realization that I'd never asked him how he was doing. It wasn't the kind of question you asked your father. He always wanted us to believe that everything would be okay. During Mom's early bout with cancer and Cliff's emerging illness, Dad kept a tight rein on our little tragedies. It was as though he was trying to dam up that flood of events that can befall a family.

It was during Dad's medical issues that I asked if he'd like to start taking some drives around town so he could get out of the house. We took Sunday drives, making stops at the house where I was born, and the apartment we lived in while our new house was being built. One time we drove out to one of the pueblos west of the city, stopping on the way to get a pecan roll at a roadside diner.

He sometimes spoke of his childhood growing up in a Texas prairie town and living in his mother's old dark house, which she kept curtained and battened down to keep out the heat. He then told me about the horror of witnessing his father's death moments after a car accident blocks from his house when he was nine-years-old.

Not long after our weekend drives, Dad suffered the first of three strokes and contracted pneumonia, which would change everything.

* * *

My wife Rose, with our baby boy in her lap, sits next to me in the visitor's room digesting what the doctor had said about my Dad's condition: "Jack's had a series of transient ischemic attacks—in short—mini strokes. While they can lead to more serious strokes, I think it's more important to focus on the pneumonia. He's very weak and not respond-ing well to the antibiotics, as we had hoped. He's on a ventilator so you need to take it slow as you talk to him."

Rose volunteers to see him first, allowing me time to compose my thoughts and try to figure what I can say to him. I search hopelessly for the right words.

In this moment I'm aware, not for the first time, that Rose is stronger than I am. She will hold his hand, and I can imagine him closing his eyes as he listens to someone who truly touches his heart. And she'll pray for him in a warm, reassuring way that has no strings or conditions attached, and she'll stroke his forehead gently and kiss his brow, just as she would a child.

I hold my year-old son in my lap and cradle him against my jacketed chest—waiting. I whisper little messages to him and kiss his head every now and then. His fine hair still has that wonderful baby smell. I think of the irony of how one life ends and another begins in a strangely cyclical pattern. I wonder if, as my son has no memory of being born, so too Dad will have no memory of this world when he's left it. But this train of thought soon spirals into an unending tangle of logic and probabilities that I haven't the energy to follow. I only know that somehow, I must distill some meaning out of this moment.

The visitor's room is as you'd expect. On the end tables, magazine covers depict political agendas or beauty secrets. In one corner of the fluorescently lighted room, a family of six is talking all at once in Spanish, as though they were at home in their kitchen. The teenage son wears an oversize football jersey. He stands behind his seated father, occasionally slapping him affectionately on the shoulder. An older daughter cradles an infant to her breast and rocks it gently. The mother delicately combs several strands of hair out of her younger daughter's face as she listens to the girl tell her something very important. Watching them interacting, laughing, even teasing each other suddenly makes me feel very sad.

Rose is beside me reaching for my son's upraised arms.

"Honey, he looks so frail. But you can tell from his eyes that he's aware. His eyes registered when I talked with him. They smiled . . . his eyes smiled."

The sounds of the room recede as I begin the long journey to his room. The corridor is empty except for the occasional medical apparatus parked against the wall. I step around an abandoned laundry cart stuffed with bedding. The hallway is stark and illuminated by the unnatural light more common to bunkers and institutional mazes deep underground.

Hyperventilating, I see the narrow channel before me is littered with the ghostly wreckage of our past. Disappointment, judgment, pride, give way to a deep longing to recover what we've lost.

So maybe this is how you salvage the love between a son and his dying father. Perhaps you begin . . .

"Dad, do you remember—?"

THE GREAT LEVELER

I first heard the expression "The Great Leveler" in my senior year of high school. Toward the end of the term, a handful of teachers, running short on lessons and the energy to deliver them, arranged for their students to watch the film *To Kill a Mockingbird*. They packed us into the school's small auditorium and projected the film over two consecutive afternoons.

If you haven't seen the movie, or read Harper Lee's novel upon which it is based, *Mockingbird* tells the story of a southern lawyer who, while raising two motherless children, defies the prejudices of the community in which they live to defend a Black man wrongly accused of raping a white woman.

The film has been lauded by both the film community and the public, and it's likely you've seen at least a snippet of its fine courtroom scene. Here is the great Gregory Peck as Atticus Finch—in that white suit and horn-rimmed glasses—delivering his summation to the jury. In a power-fully restrained performance, Peck frames his argument with the declaration that "In this country, our courts are the Great Levelers . . ."

At first, I wasn't sure I knew what this meant, but it seemed to fit very nicely on the side of *justice*. Eventually, The Great Leveler came to mean "equalizer" to me; that is, something that renders all things equal in whichever context you place them. With *Mockingbird*, it meant that in the marble face of America's judicial system, all people are judged equally, without prejudice.

The Great Leveler stayed in my consciousness for years, gathering more and more significance as I followed the civil rights movement, witnessed the final days of the Vietnam War—fought primarily by working class soldiers without college deferments—shuddered in disbelief at Watergate, and recognized the absurdity of trickle-down economics in a nation where the division between rich and poor was ever widening. These were clearly examples of a Great Un-leveling.

I've carried Harper Lee's definition of American justice through two or three careers, a very happy marriage; the gratification of being a parent; and a world that still struggles with political, social, and economic inequality.

Earlier this week, I scheduled a business trip to work on a marketing video for a client. I departed my home in the Southwest, with its intense UV rays and fifty-mile line-of-sight in every direction, and arrived in the East, under cover of the storybook woods of Washington, D.C.

Here, the lush greenery is pierced now and again by gleaming white monuments, government edifices, palatial homes and townhouses, and monolithic corporate head-quarters that spread opulently across some of the most expensive real estate in the country.

Having rented a car at the airport, I missed my turnoff and found myself inching along Leesburg Pike to get to my hotel at Tyson's Corner, Virginia. Somewhere between traffic lights I remembered how badly I needed to get some things laundered.

It's then that I began what seemed like a medieval quest to find a laundromat. I'd long given up on my hotel reforming its "guest laundry service," having had several bad experiences with missing clothes, forcing me to deliver a marketing presentation without any socks.

Now, if you've ever been inside the Beltway—the highway named for its loop around Washington, D.C.—something that may strike you is how few signs there are hugging the streets, whether from the loop or along the main thoroughfares connecting some of the more exclusive burgs. Apparently, the zoning laws prohibit businesses from ostentatiously displaying their signs, advertisements, shields, logos, or marquees.

You may drive past an eatery three or four times before you realize it's not what you thought was a dentist's office. Eventually, you spot the little green neon sign in cursive text over the entrance: Lin's Chinese Cuisine. This must be how our Founding Fathers envisioned it.

What's more, as you pass strip malls, specialty stores, and the occasional huge subdivision that looks like a stretch of *Monopoly* houses between Boardwalk and Pacific Avenue, you find yourself longing for any vestige of the mundane, the dilapidated, or even the condemned. At every intersection, you glance in both directions, hoping perversely to spy a burned-out storefront or an empty lot strewn with tires, bricks, and bottles.

About the time I resolved to call off the search, I made a spontaneous right turn off Route 7 onto a residential street. As soon as I straightened out the wheel, the most wonderful two-lane, winding street opened up before me, bordered on both sides by two-story, colonial brick houses. One house sported a window box containing lovely white flowers near the front porch where an Adirondack chair waited expectantly for an occupant in a cardigan sweater. A tricycle lay on its side in the gravel driveway.

Beside another house I glimpsed a clothesline waving its brightly-colored flags in the late summer breeze. Beneath it, a teenage boy pushed an old-fashioned lawn mower along a tiny square of Kentucky bluegrass, carefully ducking his head beneath the wires strung between metal posts. He wore an audio headset and moved the mower like a dance partner.

After an excruciatingly slow drive past extravagant homes and offices and townhouses, the view opening before me seemed like Shangri-La, though it was as common and unassuming as *Mister Rogers' Neighborhood*. And there, at the end of this meandering street, I beheld the most beautiful sight: a Ford pickup, circa 1950, resting on cinder blocks in a driveway. The rust and corrosion where the body met the chassis looked like dried blood around a gaping wound. It was a signpost for the real world.

The street came to an abrupt end at a perpendicular road lined with small businesses serving the neighborhood. The brick storefronts must have been attractive at some time long past; they'd been fashioned to a decidedly colonial look like most everything in this part of the city. But now the bricks were chipped or missing in places or bore the stamp of taggers here and there.

Beside two vacant storefronts stood my Holy Grail— the Liberty Bell Laundry.

I hesitate to mention that I kind of like laundromats. Maybe it's the soothing rumble of the churning and rotating machines or the pungent combination of steamy air and laundry soap. (As a child, I used to draw a chair up to our top-loading washing machine and, with the lid open, stare hypnotically at the agitator. I should ask a therapist friend of mine just what that could mean.)

As an adult, I guess I enjoy being surrounded by the dynamics of people working things out in their day-to-day living. Sometimes it's a mother chasing an out-of-control toddler around the laundry folding tables or a lover squabbling with his partner on his cell phone. In any case, it never ceases to be captivating.

By the first rinse cycle of my washing machine, my attention was drawn from a two-year old copy of *People* magazine to a tall figure entering the laundromat with a briefcase and a garbage bag full of laundry.

He had to be six-foot something, and he wore a carefully tucked Armani shirt with the sleeves rolled up one cuff's length, a pair of neatly creased slacks, and Forzieri leather loafers with tassels and no socks.

You'll notice that I toss these brand names about like I can easily discern fine men's fashion from the department store brands I wear; but when you travel as much as I do, you can almost commit to memory all the catalog items displayed in the in-flight magazines stuffed into the seat pocket in front of you.

Of course, the shirt was open at the neck, revealing a nest of dark hair over an "airbrush-perfect" copper tan. His expression revealed some uncertainty, as if he'd just walked into a monster truck rally.

Approaching a row of washers, he set his briefcase down on the top-loading machine and emptied the contents of the garbage bag into the tub. Almost as an afterthought, he stared at the coin tray mechanism then down into the washer full of clothes.

Thumbing through his wallet, he pulled out a twenty-dollar bill and searched his surroundings for a coin machine. He spotted one at the rear of the shop, clearly displaying a five-dollar bill and a one-dollar bill above the coin catcher.

Stiffly, the man approached the laundry attendant, who was folding large blankets and rugs near the back of the shop.

"Can you change a twenty?"

The attendant looked up at the man, then at the twenty-dollar bill as if it were a piece of lint, then turned his attention back to his monotonous task.

"You'll have to get change at the 7-Eleven. I don't keep lots of cash on hand."

"Where's the 7-Eleven?" the customer asked.

"Next block up, same side of the street," the attendant replied.

It was then that I noticed a short, stocky woman, maybe five feet tall. Her thick black, gray-streaked hair was pulled back into a colorful scarf. I could tell from her forearms that she'd done hard work. Briefly standing upright over her load of wash, she turned and called out.

"How many quarters you need? Washers are a buck; dryers seventy-five cents. The soap machine takes dollar bills if you got 'em."

"Let's see, I don't know, two, maybe three dollars in quarters? Then I'll need some one-dollar bills," he said.

"Here, here," she said, eyeballing the amount of the coins and bills she pulled from her purse. "Give me the twenty."

"Right."

After purchasing the detergent, the man looked around cautiously, then propped his briefcase on the edge of the washer and emptied what looked like socks and underwear and what I'd swear was a woman's blouse into the hungry tub. Finally, he punched a hole in a mini box of detergent with his thumb and spread the contents gingerly over his clothes as if he were seasoning a salad.

After checking the status of my washing, my attention turned back to the man as I heard him take a call on his silver, clam-sized flip phone. As if suddenly changing characters in a play, he now spoke loudly and confidently—clearly interested in allowing all the laundry patrons to take in his conversation.

His voice took on the gravity of Mark Antony's speech to the Romans following Caesar's assassination. But instead of saying, "I come to bury Caesar, not to praise him," he growled into the phone: "This Clawson acquisition is tanking. I don't know who did the due diligence on this thing, but even the shareholders were squawking at the last quarterly con call. Look, we either buy them to kill our competition, or we take advantage of the best of their products and services . . . Yes, yes, that's right . . . Reach out to Wiggins and see if he can go back over their financial statements."

He closed his flip phone and swung around, pivoting on one heel to see if anyone noticed his conversation. Apparently, no one was much interested in the Clawson acquisition.

Later, this bravado was brought down a notch or two as he carried his damp clothes across the laundry to one of the vacant dryers. After his second trip, the short woman used her foot to push her empty rolling laundry basket in his direction.

"I'm done with this," she said. "Oh yeah, and the heater setting thingy's broken on dryer number six. Fry your clothes big time."

As the man moved his clothes to the next vacant dryer, the stocky gal joined him to make sure he'd know what to do.

"Is that a silk shirt you're putting in there?" she asked.

"Yes, of course it's silk. It's an Armani—a very expensive shirt." (See, what did I tell you?)

"OK. Just think you wouldn't want to tear it up like that."

"So, I shouldn't dry this?"

She grabbed the wadded-up shirt out of his hand and quickly located the label. Holding it up for him to see, she said, "Dry clean. Dry clean only." She shook the shirt with each syllable. "Better hang it up to dry and then iron it—'course it may be too late."

Setting the shirt aside, the man collected himself and tried to finish loading the dryer. Thinking the ordeal was almost over, he was a little shaken when the woman spoke up again.

"You clean the filter?"

"Well, no—I—"

She pushed him aside, reached inside the dryer, and yanked the lint filter out of the machine.

"Here, just clean it out like this," she said as she demonstrated how to remove the lint. "You got no idea what stuff gets put in these machines."

She scraped out the contents of the filter, rolled it up into a tight ball and, without looking, tossed it into a garbage can five feet away (it would have been a three-pointer in basketball). Shaking the filter a couple of times for emphasis, she added, "tissues, gum, string, other things you don't even wanna think about."

She slipped the filter back into place. This interaction went on for some time, with the woman offering the man additional advice or tidbits from the Laundry Tree of Knowledge.

Presently, another customer shuffled slowly into the

laundromat from the side street entrance. She held her tattered overcoat tightly to her body and tipped her ragged knit cap as a greeting to the laundry attendant, who approached her respectfully.

"Queen Cleo! How are you my friend?" he said in a most pleasant voice. I was mildly surprised how his tone was much different than it had been with Mr. Armani.

"Fit as a fiddle, as my Granny used to say! How're you, Randy?" she returned.

The woman appeared to be in her 50s, although the burden of being homeless may have added years to her appearance. Her shoeless feet were bound up in pieces of cloth tied in multiple places.

"Come on back, Cleo," the attendant said. "I've washed and dried those two big blankets you brought in this morning."

Mr. Armani, the stocky woman, and others looked on discreetly, while engaged in their own business.

Cleo followed Randy several steps behind, keeping a comfortable distance between them. Placing her hand between the folds of one blanket on the folding table, she said, "They're still warm. Wish they could stay that way."

Randy said, "So, are you spending much time at the shelter?"

"I do, sort of, but there's some bad stuff there," she said looking down at the floor.

"So sorry, Cleo."

Randy reached into a plastic laundry basket sitting beneath the table with a crudely marked label that read, "Lost and Found," and produced a pair of used running shoes.

He turned toward Cleo and said, "Hey, listen, do you know of anyone who could wear a size 10½ men's running shoe?" He held them up for her to see. "No one's claimed them and it's been about two weeks."

Cleo touched the top of one sneaker and said, "There's two or three in my camp might could use 'em."

"They're yours for the taking. Hope someone gets some use out of them," Randy replied.

Cleo took the shoes and smiled faintly. The laundry attendant picked up the two blankets and said, "Let me help you with these. Got your basket outside?"

She nodded and said, "I do." As she approached the side door, she turned and tipped her knit hat again as a salutation to Randy or maybe to the laundromat itself.

The attendant followed her outside and helped her organize her grocery basket of belongings.

While I finished gathering up my clothes to leave, a huge basket of dirty laundry appeared at the front entrance of the laundromat with a chubby man half behind and half under it. Mr. Armani stopped placing his newly-laundered clothes into his garbage bag, took a broad step in the new customer's direction, and pulled the door open for him.

After a quick "thanks," the man set the basket down on the nearest folding table with a heavy breath. He had an agitated look about him, as if maybe he'd just lost the family vacation money at the casino. His small dark eyes darted all around the place, sizing things up. With his clip-on sunglasses in the up position, he started frantically patting his pockets for change and finally produced his wallet. Sweat beaded on his balding head and his shirt was already showing damp rings under the arms.

Mr. Armani approached the vacationer and said mildly, "I've got some leftover change if you need it. Mostly dollar bills."

With Mr. Armani towering over the vacationer, the transaction was made. As he thanked Mr. Armani a second time, I couldn't help but think that he looked rather like the visibly shaken rabbit with the pocket watch in *Alice in Wonderland*.

On his way out, Mr. Armani offered some kindly advice to the vacationer.

"Stay clear of dryer number six. It'll fry your clothes," he said politely, adding "—big time." And he was gone.

That night, in my colonial-furnished hotel room overlooking the Beltway, I smiled at the laundry episode and pondered its meaning. I realized that there are great levelers among us in the most unexpected places. They are etched in my psyche as clear as the words of Dr. Martin Luther King, Jr. from a speech I once read of his Integrated Schools address in 1959:

> Make a career of humanity. Commit yourself to the noble struggle for equal rights. You will make a better person of yourself, a greater nation of your country, and a finer world to live in.

Who'd have thought that the community inside the Liberty Bell Laundry would meet the attributes of a Great Leveler?

MARTIN SEES DOUBLE

Martin exited the theater with twenty or thirty other moviegoers and, stepping down the sloped entrance under the marquee, was blinded by the late afternoon sun. He squinted until his vision started to clear.

Downtown Albuquerque looked deserted on Sundays. The banks, the law offices, the gas and electric companies, the music store, the women's apparel shops were all closed. Looking to the left, Martin saw a couple of people loitering around Lindy's Diner at the corner of Fifth Street and Central Avenue, one leaning against the window reading a newspaper, the other digging through the trash for discarded bottles and other treasures. To Martin's right, an old woman waited at the bus stop on a wooden bench, searching deep in her handbag for something.

Martin expected his ride between 4:00 and 4:15. He normally would have driven himself, but his dad was having the car serviced. He'd arranged for his high school buddy Palmer to pick him up.

Martin lingered around the theater entrance, gazing occasionally at the lobby cards and movie stills in the glass cases. He thought of how satisfying it was that he was oftentimes unpredictable to his friends and contrary to their teenage identities. At 18, he enjoyed attending classic film revivals, particularly if they included films by John Huston, Billy Wilder, or Alfred Hitchcock. His friends preferred popular counterculture movies like *M*A*S*H* or *Easy Rider* or *Alice's Restaurant*. They figured that movies filmed in black and white were dated and irrelevant.

Suddenly conscious that his shoulder-length blond hair was flying a bit in the breeze, Martin found the elastic hair tie in his pocket and, forming a ponytail with his hands, secured the tie in place. In 1972, he was occasionally the object of scorn and random "male or female" comments from strangers, but he weathered most of the insults indifferently.

Martin checked his watch; ten minutes had passed. He noticed a bicycle rider coming up Central on the opposite side of the street, hugging the curb expertly. He looked to be riding a ten-speed bike with downward curled handlebars. As Martin was to remember this event later, the scene decelerated into slow motion, whereupon he became acutely aware of small details happening sequentially.

He saw a large convertible with its top down come up slowly behind the cyclist. A woman on the passenger side of the front seat waved to the cyclist and yelled, "Hey, Martin! . . . Martin!"

Are they talking to me, wondered Martin? He didn't recognize the woman or the driver. The cyclist slowed to a stop beside the car and, smiling, spoke a few words that Martin could not make out. He was tall and lean, with bony elbows held at his side as he balanced the bike. His face was narrow with a strong brow and long nose supporting wire rimmed eyeglasses, and he had lengthy blond hair pulled back into a ponytail. He was a dead ringer for Martin.

The cyclist laughed a couple of times and tapped the top of the passenger's car door.

Moments later, the car continued slowly up the street. The cyclist then turned and, staring directly at Martin, gave the universal head nod and smile, as if to acknowledge that they not only knew one another—they looked like each other.

The cyclist slid his foot into the right pedal clip and propelled himself forward. Martin adjusted his own wire rimmed glasses over his nose and watched as his double rode up the street and disappeared under the railroad bridge.

Martin felt a wave of uneasiness as he replayed the scene in his head over and over. Just what are the odds of encountering someone who looks exactly like you? And what are the odds that same person shares your name? The improbability of such a coincidence was now called into question.

Martin didn't notice Palmer pulling up in his dad's Pontiac GTO and rumbling to a stop. His friend tapped the horn just to be cute, which brought Martin out of his trance. The memories of this episode would be recalled in the coming months and embellished when shared with his friends over a beer.

* * *

Between high school graduation and his fourth semester at college, Martin had become 'Marty' to his friends and acquaintances. This day he sat in the back row of his Charles Dickens college class, hoping the professor wouldn't call on him as he hadn't completed the reading assignment from the previous week.

"Mr. Martin," asked professor Boughman, "with all the characters of *Bleak House* established, and the plot slowly beginning to reveal deeper meanings, what would you say that Dickens is trying to tell us about the Court of Chancery?"

Marty inhaled deeply and flipped through the pages of the book, as if a response would magically come to him. After a painfully lengthy pause, another student raised her hand.

"Yes, Ms. Erin!"

The redheaded student in the next row sat up straight in her seat and launched into an eloquent response that began, "I think that Dickens is leading his characters to the realization that the Jarndyce and Jarndyce court case will end up consuming all of the inheritances meant for its heirs . . ."

Marty closed his paperbound copy of the voluminous novel. At that moment, a student entered the classroom and addressed the professor politely.

"Mr. Boughman, I'm a transfer from Mrs. Harding's Naturalism in Fiction course. Her class was full up, and it's taken a couple of weeks for the transfer to come through."

Startled, Marty immediately recognized the student as the cyclist he'd seen passing the movie theater several years before. He felt his heart beating in his throat.

"Ah yes, Martin!" Boughman replied. "We've been expecting you. You are, in fact, the other Martin Richards on my attendance sheet. We may have some challenges telling you apart!"

His last name is Richards, too? thought Marty incredulously.

For the benefit of the new student, the professor gestured with his hand to the general area where Marty sat in the back of the classroom. Marty looked away, trying to conceal his embarrassment. Surely other students would recognize the insanity of having two unrelated—but identical—twins in their class, with the same first and last name, too.

Weeks went by, and Marty eventually caught up with the reading assignments and enjoyed participating in class discussions. But he couldn't shake his acute awareness that it was his doppelgänger who sat in the front row of desks near the professor's lectern. The "other" still had shoulder-length hair and wire rimmed glasses, and he tended to dress in ragged, knitted sweaters and denim blue jeans.

Over time, Marty acquiesced that Martin was a good student who offered startlingly good insights on Dickens' novels. It was also apparent that other students liked him and were impressed with his intellect.

Throughout the semester, Marty carefully avoided situations in which he might have to speak to Martin either before or after class. He continually rehearsed what he might say in such an encounter and wondered whether it would be appropriate to state the obvious. In his mind, such a declaration would come across as unbalanced—bordering on creepy.

Marty's girlfriend continually chastised him for not dealing with the issue directly. "Why don't you just go up to him and say, 'hey, I couldn't help notice that we look very much alike. Might it be possible that we're related?' What's the worst that could happen?"

"Guys just don't do that, Karen," Marty explained. "If he doesn't see the resemblance, he might think I'm certifiable. I just can't do it."

"I swear, men are such little boys!" Karen replied.

No communication ever passed between the two Martins in class, and Marty went on to receive his bachelor's degree in English in May of 1976.

* * *

Marty sat comfortably in his furnished apartment on a Saturday afternoon, watching a black and white TV Western about a wagon train that seemed never to get the settlers to their destination. He had muted the audio in response to a string of advertisements and left it muted when the broadcast returned to the program.

He sat with his feet propped up on the coffee table and pushed himself more deeply into the sofa. The sofa had always had this faint odor of something he couldn't place. But right now, he was pondering the path his life had taken after college. With some effort, Marty had landed a good technical writing job with an environmental engineering firm, where he kept busy writing and editing proposals and technical reports. He'd long abandoned his intention of going to graduate school and becoming an English professor.

Marty was startled by the ring of his doorbell—something that rarely happened, as he mostly communicated with his girlfriend and other friends by phone or at scheduled get-togethers. Maybe it was the landlord, he thought.

Marty looked through the door's peephole, and his heart jumped when he spied his double standing under the eaves of the front porch. Marty backed away from the door as the doorbell rang a second time. With some trepidation, he unlocked the deadbolt and opened the door.

Martin was dressed in a turtleneck sweater and corduroy pants, and his hair was now shorter and parted stylishly down the middle. His wire rims had been replaced with tortoise shell eyeglasses, and he held what looked like a small stack of letters in his left hand.

Before the man could speak, Marty blurted out, "Oh, hey. Let me guess—from college days—right? Martin isn't it?"

"Yes! You do remember me then," Martin replied with that same knowing smile and head nod lodged in Marty's memory. Then he added, "Do you have a second?"

"Sure, sure, come on in."

After Marty invited his doppelgänger to have a seat, the latter spoke first.

"This may seem strange, but I keep getting mail that I expect may belong to you." He handed Marty the stack of four or five letters.

Marty shuffled through them, and noted, "It's my name but obviously not my address." The letters had red stamped or printed envelopes with big, bold words like PAYMENT DUE, PAST DUE, DEBT COLLECTION NOTICE.

"I realize the address isn't yours, but it was clear that I was getting someone else's mail—someone named Martin Richards. So, I got your unlisted address from the operator, telling them I was looking for my long-lost brother, and here I am."

Marty smiled at the irony and asked, "Did the operator have any other Richards' addresses on file?"

"Nope; they had no other address or phone number—other than my own."

Could it be that there was now a "third man"?

Marty brought up this new wrinkle in the situation and said, "You know what's weird? Over the past year, I've been getting threatening phone calls from angry creditors who're ready to repossess my car and place liens on my bank account. I get calls from finance companies, auto dealers, furniture stores, sporting goods stores—you name it. But I tell them over and over that they have the wrong Martin Richards. I've honestly thought about getting a lawyer to get them to cease and desist!"

Martin laughed and said, "I get the same calls, man. I've also gotten some angry recorded messages from women claiming that I'm their ex-boyfriend. I thought they were possibly for you! No offense intended."

Marty smiled slightly, shook his head, and handed the letters back to Martin. After a long pause, he offered his visitor a glass of water and mustered the courage to bring up the one subject that still troubled him.

"I don't know exactly how to say this, but you *must* be aware that we look very much alike." He hesitated, searching for some semblance of acknowledgement from Martin, but his expression conveyed nothing. "Like brothers, I mean. No, that's not quite right . . . like identical twins." Still, no response. "Does any of this register, Martin?"

The "other" put the dead letters on the coffee table and sat back in his cushioned chair. "You mean like a doppelgänger—an alter ego—an evil twin?" He smiled slyly.

Marty raised his voice in frustration, "You're not taking me seriously. Do you not see the resemblance? Same face, same eyes, same hair, same—" then he stopped.

Martin closed his eyes briefly in thought, then said, "Be cool, Marty. Let's see, how can I begin?"

Marty regained his composure and wiped his eyes as if wind had blown dust into them.

"Maybe I'm the person you always wanted to be," Martin began. "I was driven to be the best at everything I attempted. I was a joiner; in high school I went out for sports—track and field mostly; played percussion with the school marching band; joined the drama club and was in *Charley's Aunt*, *Our Town*, and *Twelve Angry Men*; oh yeah, and I belonged to the chess club."

Marty considered asking him to stop, but let it pass.

"In college, I entered a doctoral program in English and specialized in twentieth century American lit. Been teaching at New Mexico State for the past two years. But you—"

Stunned that anyone would have the audacity to make such an accusation, Marty shot back, "What gives you the right to make me out to be some kind of failure? You took your path—I took mine."

Martin's laugh carried an air of condescension, and he started to speak when Marty was jolted awake as if he were plummeting from a cliff face. The TV was broadcasting some other Western series from the 1960s, and the audio was still muted. Marty sat bolt upright and looked for the letters on the coffee table, but they were no longer there. And neither was Martin.

Marty tried to catch his breath. He'd never had a nightmare on a Saturday afternoon, and he'd never recalled a dream with such clarity.

In his mind's instant replay, he heard the same words over and over: "Maybe I'm the person you always wanted to be—maybe I'm the person you always wanted to be."

Marty got to his feet and walked into the kitchen. He leaned over the counter to peer through the blinds at the light of the day. He felt like crying but forced himself to stave off the impulse.

What the hell? he thought.

* * *

Many years passed, and Marty made a good life for himself. He married young and divorced in his late forties, but was now dating a smart and pretty woman named Maggie

Walsh. In 2012, he'd become a training manager for a solar engineering firm, had earned several promotions, and had forged memorable friendships with some of his coworkers. On any given day, he never took for granted that he worked in a healthy environment, where people enjoyed collaborating with each other.

On Sunday, Marty and Maggie planned to take advantage of spring break and ride their bikes through the university campus. Before their ride, Marty dropped by a local bike shop he'd heard about to have his twenty-one-speed checked over and the tires inflated.

In the shop, several employees were helping other patrons with their bikes. A fellow who looked like he could be the shop owner, glanced up and said, "Be right with you."

Marty dropped the kickstand on his bike and waited patiently. The "might-be" shop owner approached and said, "Ah, nice bike! One of the best hybrids on the market. What can I do for you?"

"Thought I'd do some riding this afternoon," Marty said, "but figured I should get the tires inflated correctly and maybe have the bike checked out. I've got an air pump at home, but I never know how many pounds of pressure to put in each tire."

Marty looked at the man and felt as though he seemed vaguely familiar.

The man said, "Hybrid tires generally range from 40 to 70 psi. You ride mostly on the street?"

"Yes—almost exclusively," Marty replied.

"We'll take care of it, and I'd be happy to lubricate the drivetrain, check your brake system, and tighten some of the hardware if you like."

"That'd be great."

While the specialist worked on his bike, Marty studied

the man's face, particularly the eyes, and finally realized who he was.

"Excuse me, you look really familiar. Did you go to UNM? Maybe take a Charles Dickens course?"

The man looked up from testing the tension on the bicycle chain and said, "I did. I did! God, that must have been, what, 1974, '75?"

"Yes! I had the same class—with Mr. Boughman," Marty replied.

The man stood up with the can of WD-40 in one hand, and reached out the other to shake Marty's hand. "I'm Martin Richards."

"And I'm Martin Richards too, only I go by Marty."

"This is crazy-weird," Martin said, shaking his head and smiling. "The professor had one hell of a time keeping us apart. You know, I still read those mammoth novels. I'm reading *War and Peace* right now, and it's kicking my butt!"

Marty laughed and finally understood that their once startling resemblance had changed somehow. The man before him had put on a little weight, his face was rounder, and while his hair was still long, the hairline was receding on his forehead. A bald spot was also starting to show. He no longer wore glasses, which implied either that he wore contacts or had had LASIK surgery.

Marty said, "I still do a good bit of reading when I find the time. Never tackled Tolstoy, but Victor Hugo is my nemesis. I swear that I'll get through *Les Misérables* before I die."

Martin finished giving Marty's bike a quick maintenance check and said, "Listen Marty, please come see us again. I started the shop with a friend back in '86, and we've got some of the best bike mechanics in the city."

"Will do, Martin. Good bumping into you again. I'll bring my girlfriend's bike in sometime soon. She actually takes much better care of hers than I do mine."

As Marty lifted his bike into the back of his hatchback, he thought back to the first time he'd seen his double riding a ten-speed up Central Avenue across from the downtown theater. So, Martin's life had come full circle with his bike shop.

Marty looked up at the sign over the shop, which read, *Two Guys Bike Stop*. He smiled, closed the tailgate, and drove to Maggie's house near the university campus.

FROM THE LOWER FORTY-EIGHT

We flew the 280 miles from Anchorage, Alaska to Kodiak Island on a starless night, rain pounding the windows and updrafts tossing the twin-engine plane about like an amusement ride.

When we landed, visibility was still limited, and we hunched our shoulders up to keep the rain off the backs of our necks as we walked single file from the plane to the terminal.

The station's interior had a damp, organic feel to it, with wildlife and Air Alaska posters gracing the walls and passengers trying to dry out before boarding flights back to the mainland. The food court comprised two vending machines, but I think we were hungrier to get to our motel than to consume more packaged snacks.

Kim and I had traveled from the Midwest to attend a course titled A History of Labor Unions in America. That our earliest opportunity to catch the training was in Alaska was a lucky accident; as tenured professors of Sociology, we often found ourselves attending courses and conferences on college campuses or in dense urban centers. Kodiak was a welcome exception.

At the car rental counter, the agent handed me the keys to a fifteen-year-old sedan rather than the all-wheel drive vehicle we hoped would handle any terrain. Since neither of us had a reliable GPS system on our flip phones, we grabbed what looked like a Triple A map that had been buried in a glove compartment for over a decade. One side displayed a map of the entire island, the other the city of Kodiak.

Before edging our car out of the parking lot onto the two-lane road, a heavily jacketed fellow, blinking rapidly to keep the rain out of his eyes, told us we'd find our lodging one block west of the one traffic light in town. I rolled up the window and gave Kim my "here goes nothin'" expression, and we disappeared into a tunnel of darkness.

We drove a few miles in silence. Silvery threads of rain continued to dash against the windshield between the groaning wipers. I maintained a steady speed and kept a tight focus on the road ahead, or what little of it I could make out. No matter which direction we looked, there wasn't anything resembling topography—just darkness. We could have been in the desert, in a mountain pass, or chugging across the Sea of Tranquility on the moon.

"Surely, we'll see the traffic light?" Kim said.

"God, I hope so. I should have been watching the odometer. The agent said about five miles to the intersection, right?

"That's what I heard," Kim said as she adjusted the defroster to improve our visibility.

"I'm afraid if I go much faster, we'll hydroplane. It feels like there isn't any tread on the dang tires." To lighten the mood, I added, "You don't suppose they'll find us in the morning stranded and parked thirty feet from the post office?"

She laughed, which reassured me that we were both okay.

The traffic signal turned out to be a flashing yellow light, and we both jumped when we saw a pedestrian in the crosswalk not ten feet from the car. There were no signs of distress, just a person out for a stroll—in the middle of a torrent.

What I remember most about the motel was that the shaggy carpeted floors were kind of uneven and there were two or three places where you had to step up or step down as if the builders hadn't quite made up their minds. But the desk clerk made us feel very welcome and looked sympathetic for what I imagined were our exhausted expressions and sagging posture.

The travel day ended with my rather feeble, "Good night . . . Shall we meet in the breakfast room around 7:00?" and we took separate corridors to our rooms.

* * *

When I used to travel for work, the sun would invariably wake me before the radio alarm would go off. But on this first morning in Alaska, I opened my eyes to what felt like a cavern. I stumbled to the window to find that the rain had continued through the night; it was still dark outside— very dark.

Over coffee and fruit in a breakfast nook near the motel's front desk, Kim and I laughed about our little adventure the night before and how weird it felt waking up to darkness.

"Before we left LAX, I checked online, and it said it wouldn't be light until mid-morning," she said.

We were on the road soon after breakfast, once again traveling blind in the rain. We followed a winding two-lane road that passed warehouses and other nondescript, unmarked buildings. We then pulled up to what looked like a wide paved highway preceded by a sign that said, CAUTION, ACTIVE RUNWAY — Low Flying Aircraft.

"Oh man," I said. "I remember Greg said there's supposed to be a Coast Guard airstrip near the convention center. They fly big cargo planes and helicopters on search and rescue missions from here."

"Yikes! We'll have to cross it to get to the training site," Kim said. "Gun it!"

I wiped my eyes, squinted to the left, then the right, and punched the accelerator, hoping a C-130 aircraft didn't come barreling down the runway.

A short time after, we reached the Kodiak Convention Center and were greeted warmly by the instructors and other attendees from parts unknown. We participated in an interesting—if somewhat routine—training session before the leader called for a brief recess.

"People, you'll be happy to know the sun's out and the rain has stopped! Let's be back in fifteen."

There was practically a stampede to the front doors. For the first time, Kim and I beheld the landscape we'd traversed the night before.

A Coast Guard cutter with the classic white hull and red vertical stripe near the bow was docked in the harbor among smaller civilian vessels. To the north we could see a range of jagged snow-capped peaks. The air was clean and fresh—an aromatic mixture of ocean, wet soil, and early winter foliage. On the opposite side of the expanse, we could see small, forested, emerald islands with small whitecaps surging at their bases.

During an extended lunch hour, we took a short drive

around the town and discovered wonderfully charming homes and small businesses surrounding the many coves, nestled up against evergreen trees. Downtown, among the newer properties, older shops bore wooden signs displaying bears and other wildlife or marine images.

Our attention was piqued by a Russian Orthodox church with blue onion-shaped domes, bounded by a white picket fence. As we were to learn later, the church and the numerous Russian street names, like Kouskov and Ismailov, signaled that the Russians had once occupied Kodiak because of the abundant hunting grounds and bustling trade routes. Their control of the island ended in 1867.

* * *

Our final day of training ended at noon, leaving me and Kim nearly half the day to do some exploring. Our flight back home would leave in the morning.

We dropped into a local eatery recommended by the training lead for good comfort food and a rustic ambiance. We found the place packed and were escorted to seats at the bar, where we struck up a conversation with a friendly fellow with a terra-cotta sun face and salt and pepper beard.

"You come from the lower forty-eight, do you?" he inquired.

Kim smiled and said, "My goodness, does it show?"

"Meant no offense. You just look maybe like you ain't from around here." He smiled then added, "I kind of figured, since you didn't have your camo and field boots on or a six-point bull elk tied to the roof of your vehicle . . . Name's Jerry."

We laughed, and Kim replied, "We're both college professors from Iowa, which is kind of *down under* when you think of how far north Kodiak is from the Midwest!"

Turned out Jerry worked for the U.S. Fish & Wildlife Service and claimed to know the island better than just about anyone.

"We've got the afternoon off and thought we'd tool around the town," I said. "Do you have any recommendations for a couple of out-of-towners?"

"There's only about a hundred miles of road on this entire island, but there's a good one that'll take you 'round a series of bays where you might see some birds and land animals—rock sandpipers or yellow-billed loons, for instance, and maybe a bear or two. It's all real pretty country."

Jerry then explained how most of the west end of the island was only accessible by boat or seaplane, in large part out of respect for the indigenous tribes that had been living there for thousands of years, and to serve as a wildlife refuge.

After lunch, we drove southwest, following the road as far as it would take us. For the next few hours, moving through a Kodiak-scape of golden hills and beautiful shallows where the bay water lapped against the tall grass, Kim and I talked about everything from careers, the joys and challenges of parenting, and the high costs of a college education, to things we liked to do outside of work.

I remember thinking at that moment how wonderful it was to get to know my colleague better through our shared experience, and I realized we'd both probably remember this adventure for years to come.

We had just decided to circle back to town, when Kim grabbed my arm and yelled, "A bear! I see a bear! There . . . there, just beyond that gnarled-looking bush!"

Slowing the car down, I inched forward to catch a better look. "I don't see it—Wait! There! Looks like he's pawing at something."

"I think it's a fish," Kim said. "It is a fish—he's got himself a salmon!"

The bear looked as if it was almost playing with the fish—batting it around—and then bringing it up to its jaws and biting it in half.

We sat motionless in the car, transfixed but fumbling for our phone cameras, when the bear moved into deeper water with only its head visible. In a matter of moments, the bear disappeared into the shallows. We sat there thinking that we'd just seen a Kodiak bear and had no evidence to prove it.

In the morning, we drove leisurely to the airport, taking in both sides of the road and laughing about the big reveal of our trip: from total darkness to the beauty of a veritable jewel of Alaska known as Kodiak Island. On our return to the lower forty-eight states, we seemed smarter and a little bit older. And now we had a tale that could be told to friends and colleagues alike, over and over, with a bear that would undoubtedly get bigger and bigger with each re-telling.

SHORTER STORIES

KID'S STUFF

Wall walking in suburbia

Many homes in suburban Albuquerque had cinder block walls dividing homeowners' properties.

As kids, these walls presented an exciting alternative for traversing the neighborhood. Not only could we wall-walk to a friend's house, we could peer into everyone's backyard, which was intriguing—and sometimes dangerous.

For every swimming pool, kid's playhouse, back porch barbeque grill, lawn chair, and smartly manicured lawn we spied, there were angry neighbors yelling at us for violating their privacy and big, muscular dogs who behaved as if they wanted to kill us.

That's what I heard

I remember the time my Dad told me that relay runners carry the flame from Olympia to the site of the next Olympic Games, often traveling by land, sea, and air. He stressed—with a wink and a smile—that the flame is never allowed to go out.

I can't tell you how much it concerned me that the flame could be extinguished accidentally, the ramifications of which were too horrible to consider.

Sometime later, after declaring to schoolyard friends that the Olympic torch must never, ever go out, Randy Wingate looked down at my feet, shook his head, and, clasping his temples between his thumb and middle finger, said, "Kev, Kev, Kev, that's just something they say. What do you think would happen if the fire went out? Stop bein' such a goofball."

Inverted world

How many of us kids used to lay on the floor and look up at the ceiling, pretending that it was actually the floor? We imagined skirting around inverted ceiling lamps, stepping over doorways, and traipsing all through the house, looking up at bathtubs and sofas and tables and chairs overhead.

They looked like the night sky

A process for fusing glass into metal has been used through the years to fashion roasting pans, coffee pots, wash basins, and even the tubs of old washing machines. My grandmother used them and my mother used them. You've probably used them on camping trips over a campfire. Think cowboy coffee pots and cups.

Called enamelware or graniteware, these articles stimulated my youthful imagination because their blue porcelain-like surfaces and tiny white flakes reminded me of a night sky speckled with stars.

Heroes

Some people place surgeons and aerospace engineers and athletes up on pedestals. But for me, no one stood higher in my estimation than the owner of Dick's Record Roundup in an old strip mall near the intersection of San Mateo and Candelaria. I'd ride my bike over to the store, wander in, and cautiously approach the counter where the owner might be gently wiping a soft cloth over a Nat King Cole record before placing it on his turntable.

As a soundtrack collector, I'd ask him if there was a such-and-such soundtrack for a film I'd seen on TV. With a smile and a slight wink to keep the cigarette smoke out of his eyes, he'd open a huge Torah-sized catalogue book and page through it to search for the title I'd given him. Here's a typical response:

"Hmmm, 'Baby the Rain Must Fall'—I believe Mainstream records issued that soundtrack a couple years back. You know, Shorty Rogers did all the band arrangements on that record. Oh yeah—here it is. I can order this for you. By  the way, did you know that Glenn Yarbrough had a hit with that record just last year? Neely Plumb produced it."

Now that's a hero.

Store closes in ten minutes

Every Christmas, I'm reminded of a fantasy I had as a kid:

Wouldn't it be magical to be locked overnight in a department store, where you could roller skate through the aisles, stuff your face with chocolate at the candy counter, take a running jump on a row of mattresses, and—best of all—play with all the toys in the toy section? I mean, it'd be an experience of unrestrained childhood revelry.

Things go better . . .

In my youth, our family became friends and neighbors with a surgeon who'd moved his family to Albuquerque after fleeing Maoist China in the late '50s. Mrs. Luhan shared many culinary tips with my Mom over the years— which brings me to the day she filled a Coke bottle with soy sauce and walked it down to our house.

That same afternoon, I discovered the bottle on the kitchen counter, unattended. I rubbernecked left and then right, clutched it like a bootlegger, and chugged two or three gulps of what I thought would be a warm, frothy beverage. OMG.

FAMILY

"Just one more thing . . ."

When our son Josh was a young fellow, my wife and I used to devise creative ways to pass the time while waiting for our order in restaurants. On one vacation in San Diego, we made up a game whereby we pretended that employees and some of the patrons in a Shelter Island bar and grill were in an episode of Columbo.

We decided that one whiskered old fellow at the bar, with a captain's hat and red striped shirt (nursing a margarita cocktail) was the father of a woman who had gone missing.

We then pretended that the handsome pianist playing old standards with the aid of a cheesy rhythm machine in the corner had, in fact, been in love with the captain's daughter.

At the entrance to the restaurant, we figured that the tall maître d' with the black comb over (holding the menus under his arm) had been the last person to see the woman on the pier with the bank manager who was in the process of repossessing the restaurant.

By the time we had the whole plot set up, our order came. But what a fun way to pass the time waiting for dinner!

Moses and the cookie jar

There are two objects that figured prominently in our home life when we were kids, and I'm glad I still have them. Though my mother was not an overtly religious person, she studied Judaism and saw Moses as a lawgiver. She always said the subset of commandments that most people are familiar with were essentially the laws of a civilized society. She cherished this replica of Michelangelo's statue of Moses, which I bought for her after saving eleven dollars in change.

The pig cookie jar was also pivotal. Whenever my brother and I felt deserving of a reward for good behavior, we used to shout out to Mom, "Can we get a cookie from the pig?"

My brother

Today, I'm thinking about my brother, Mark, who passed away in November of 2003. Mark's life was complicated and difficult—not of his own doing—but he was a lovely person. I remember him building a home chemistry lab in our garage, where he would entertain the neighborhood kids creating smoke bombs, Borax crystal snowflakes, invisible ink, and more. Not long after that, he immersed himself in Shakespeare; philosophy; psychology; and the music of Mahler, Beethoven, and Shostakovich, while most teenagers were listening to The Beatles and The Rolling Stones.

He was my best man at our wedding, a delightful uncle to my son, Josh, and a frequent companion at New Mexico Symphony concerts I attended with my wife, Mary.

Although there were many, I will recount one experience that defined the content of Mark's character. On the day my father died, Mark went to the convalescent home where my Dad had been living and had Thanksgiving dinner with my Dad's roommate, a man suffering with early dementia and who had no relatives or visitors on this holiday.

The Shalako

I guess I was around twelve at the time (my brother, fifteen). Mom and Dad drove our family out to Zuni Pueblo, thirty miles south of Gallup, the railway town where my Mom grew up.

The dusk was bitter cold, and our shoes crackled atop the snow cover extending across the mesa. We were ushered into a home, where Native children and other family members sat against the walls of the central living space. In the center of the room stood the Shalako—an inert, towering, cone-shaped costume with a beaked mask and feathered headdress.

One hour passed in silence. The heat in the room was palpable, owing to the fire in the iron stove and the number of people huddled tightly inside the space.

Then, to the delighted screams of the children, the Shalako rose from the floor and the person inside the costume began dancing across the room, with his moccasins now clearly visible. The dance lasted for about thirty minutes, after which the Shalako once again rested on the floor.

We learned from our guide that the Shalako ceremony is a celebration of the winter solstice and the harvest, and also serves as a blessing on newly constructed homes in the pueblo.

After the ceremony, we were led by a guide to another home, where we ate tamales and drank hot chocolate.

Mom

My Mom was an amazing person. She was a straight-A student through public school, fluent in Spanish, capable of playing the piano and the Hawaiian lap guitar, an avid reader, a Sunday school teacher, ace bridge player, and a singer of old western songs, such as "Ragtime Cowboy Joe," "Tumbling Tumbleweeds," "El Paso," and countless other folksy tunes, which she'd sing with me and my brother on long road trips to California or Arizona, or just to Chama, New Mexico.

My favorite memory of her is one winter when I was probably ten- or twelve-years-old. It had just snowed, and we had family over to our house in the Northeast Heights. I recall throwing snowballs with my friends in front of our house, glancing up and seeing her standing at the window in our kitchen with the warm light shining out onto the snow.  She looked happier than any other time I can remember. Her name was Florence, but friends called her Flo.

CHRISTMASTIME

Like it was yesterday

Parking the cars, hugs and handshakes, Patsy Cline record on the stereo, family room with a small black-and-white TV blasting a football game, blue cigar and pipe smoke hovering in the air, framed Currier & Ives print at the end of the hall, out-of-tune upright piano, the uncle who used to play golf with Glen Campbell, the favorite aunt who sells Native American jewelry in Old Town, Mogen David sweet wine, Budweiser beer, hot chocolate, a box of Buffett's candies, my *Famous Monsters of Filmland* fan magazine and sketching tablet, my brother's Zenith transistor AM radio with a single earphone.

Christmas 1964.

Slideshow

I set up the slide projector and screen in my parents' living room.

Grandmother: "Oh, lookee there. Petrified Forest. There's Aunt Jetty with Ronny."

Mom: "Mother, I think that's Bobby, not Ronny. Ronny was in training at Ft. Sill in South Carolina."

Dad: "Honey, that's not the Petrified Forest. Look behind them. Those are the mountains on the edge of the Mojave Desert. That would have been back in '63 when we all went to Disneyland."

Grandmother: "No Jay, that's Arizona, I'm sure of it. There's the hood of your Oldsmobile. You had that other car on our trip to California. The Mercury."

Grandfather (looking resigned and quite relaxed): "Young fella (me), could you get me another small glass of sherry? This is gonna take a while."

Me: "Sure, Granddad."

Christmas 1974.

Our own Christmas Carol

In 2020, my wife and I were visited by three ghosts:

The Ghost of Christmas Past: Last week, a Gas Company technician "red tagged" our old stove as too dangerous to operate.

The Ghost of Christmas Present: The plumber is here fixing a problem with the thermocouple on our hot water heater.

The Ghost of Christmas Yet to Come: The appliance company technician will come to deliver and install our brand-new stove—eventually.

TWENTY-SOMETHING

I never believed in UFOs—except for five minutes in 1976

A college party—a kegger to be exact—found twenty or thirty of us milling around the backyard of a friend's house near the University of New Mexico. It was a frigid November, and we were all jacketed in our threadbare winter coats, talking and drinking beer as we watched the full moon continue its ascent in the eastern sky.

Looking west, three or four of us saw a triangular, metallic-looking object darting in and out of the dark horizon of trees and rooftops. It fired straight up, shot straight down, then rocketed parallel to the landscape. We found ourselves hyperventilating and making mumbling noises of disbelief.

Then a partier approached us, presumably to observe the same phenomenon. He said, "You know what that is, right?"

No comment.

"It's a kite. There's a group of kite pilots west of the university who fly their kites on weekend nights. I've seen their silvery, semi-transparent kites flying in the full moon, and it's trippy when the light hits 'em. Cheers."

Count me in

We college friends decided it was time to look for
alternative things to do together, apart from hiking,
drinking herbal teas and listening to music, collectively
preparing a meal, or tossing the Frisbee.

We ended up at the University of New Mexico Student
Union ballroom, where a young non-fiction author was
giving a lecture about his new book.

We entered the hall, found seats together, and sat quietly
before the lecturer took the podium. Within the first
three minutes of his painfully dry delivery, I scanned the
audience, looked at the stains on the walls, and noticed
that someone had scraped the letters on the back of the
chair in front of me, which now read *S n o t* instead of
Samsonite.

It's then that I realized I wasn't clear about the topic of
this lecture, and the rambling from the podium wasn't
helping any. I leaned over to my friend, Augie.

"Hey Aug, what was the subject of this lecture, again?"

Augie: "Ten Steps Toward Better Listening."

Albuquerque's Western Skies

Our band had won a battle-of-the-bands competition and funds to make a very low-budget music video. So, we drove out East Central to the Western Skies Hotel—a crumbling and downright ghostly lodge whose heyday had long since passed. There, we hauled lights, camera equipment, and props (including a rotary telephone and a dismembered mannequin) up a circular staircase to a remote room in the complex. We scoped out the room, with its mottled shag carpet, black tuck and roll furniture, and really funky bathroom fixtures.

JFK, Marilyn Monroe, and probably Abe Lincoln were known to have stayed there, but the place was now barely operational and serviced by a skeleton crew of young people who seemed happy to have our company. We never encountered any other guests.

If I didn't know better, I'd swear that the Eagles' "Hotel California" was written expressly for this sad and creepy establishment. Still, it served us well for our video and we were able to both check out and leave . . .

WESTERN SKIES

Focus . . . focus . . . squirrel!

In the early 1980s, I was working forty-eight weeks out of the year playing keyboards in a rock band. In the dance clubs, we often played four sets a night, five or six nights a week. Though we loved performing, this regimen could be exhausting. Then, there was this:

Over time, you become so familiar with the songs you're playing that your mind starts to wander during a performance. Maybe you're thinking about getting your car fixed or how you're going to pay the increase in your rent. Then you snap to reality when you realize you're hopelessly lost: Did we already play the second verse? Are we on the first or second chorus? Did Doug play his guitar solo?

As expected, pandemonium breaks loose. Everyone in the band seems to be playing a different part of the song, and the result is a cacophony you simply can't put into words. As you look for encouragement from the audience, you realize that the couples on the dance floor look distinctly perplexed or are laughing hysterically.

DAY TO DAY

Stay frosty

Nothing quite like stepping confidently off an elevator—on the wrong floor. Any way you slice it, it's a long walk back to the elevator and its congregation of smiling riders.

Visit to the optometrist

Doctor: "OK, Mr. Hughes, I'm now going to shine a light in your eye with the luminance of a supernova.

Look up at the ceiling. Good, good. Look to your left. Look to your right. Look at the top of my left ear. Now look straight into the light as if it's an oncoming train.

Great. No signs of cataracts. We're all done!"

Stumbling out of the examination chair, I blindly reach for something to regain my balance and place my outreached hand over the optometrist's face.

Me: "Whoops—sorry doc!"

It's all just days on the calendar

I have trouble remembering dates, like holidays, anniversaries, and special occasions. I rely on post-it notes, desk calendars, and my wife to help me remember important days throughout the year. Sometimes this breaks down.

Back in 2015:

Medical staffer: "So, Mr. Hughes, you're here for your endoscopy? When did you last eat?"

Me: "Dinner . . . night before last."

Medical staffer: "And you didn't have any meds last night, correct?"

Me: "That's right."

Medical staffer: ". . . Um, are you aware Mr. Hughes that today's your birthday?"

Me: ". . . Uh, yeah. Kinda funny how that worked out."

Testify

My wife and I have almost perfected the ability to have a conversation from opposite ends of the house. But every now and then this communication thread hits a snag.

My wife: "Remember, I'm going to have lunch with Alice on Thursday after my PT session and you'll need to get yourself something to eat."

Me: "Umm . . . (leaning forward like a mob boss testifying into a microphone at a Senate subcommittee hearing) . . . I have no recollection of that."

Comforts of home

Busy, busy at work for year's end. But at home, I find myself feeling really calm and mellow, which is so welcome at this time of year. Then I notice a small device plugged into a wall socket in our living room.

Me: "Honey, what's this? Is this one of those plug-in air fresheners?"

My wife: "Oh, that—no, that's a synthetic pheromone delivery system. It's supposed to help calm pets that experience anxiety."

The importance of being consistent

My wife is an exemplary organizer. Periodically, she patiently walks me through every cabinet, every shelf, every drawer, and the countertop to help me learn where to place clean crockery, cutlery, and other kitchen articles for easy access.

While we acknowledge that I am generally pretty consistent in placement, we have discovered that I never put the potato peeler or whisk back in the same place twice. In fact, whenever the said instruments are desired, we spend three to five minutes searching for them. We have not determined if this results from a recessive gene or some psychological predisposition, but we continue to investigate.

WORK

On the road

Our rock band had been on the road for four or five weeks and were road weary when we drove into Alamogordo, New Mexico. Our booking agent had secured some accommodations for us in several trailers on the outskirts of town.

It was Friday night when the fight broke out in the bar in which we were performing. No one knew how it started, but our sound engineer leapt into action and protected the sound board (and us) as we tried to figure out what the ruckus was all about. The owner shut down the bar shortly thereafter.

The following day, our drummer—always the voice of motherly wisdom—said we needed to go unwind and have a nice sit-down, healthy dinner at a local restaurant.

I don't recall the name of the establishment, but the staff were very friendly and asked if we'd like a beverage before ordering our meal. "Yes, a nice bottle of Chablis would suit us just fine."

We smiled in anticipation when our server arrived with the bottle of wine and proceeded to try to expel the cork with not one, but two implements designed for that purpose.

We were delighted when she looked to the right and then left and then put the bottle between her knees and yanked the cork out.

She and the band had a good laugh, and the Saturday night gig went well, without incident.

Know your audience

I had a friend and coworker many, many years ago who was once invited to give a presentation about his profession to young people at a public school. He was a colorful character and had an abundance of experiences, having been an independent journalist for *Life* magazine. The presentation went something like this:

Richard: ". . . So we went through the archives looking for everything we could find on the Warren Report and there were so many loose ends and shoddy investigations . . . There to take pictures and interview members of the Anti-Apartheid Movement . . . Grand Prix auto-race where there was a horrible collision . . . Do you all have any questions?"

Student: "How tall are you mister?"

Email by committee

Two work chums and I needed to respond to a particularly complicated situation and labored to craft the most appropriate email.

Work chum 1: "No, no, change 'meet' to 'exceed.'"

Me: "Yeah, that's good."

Work chum 2: "How about 'best intentions' rather than 'good faith'?"

Me: "Oh yeah, that's way better."

Work chum 1: "'Therefore' sounds too academic. Let's make it 'And so comma . . .'"

Work chum 2: "It's still not right . . . what else can we fix?"

Me: "I could make it rhyme."

It wasn't just the oil in the ground

I once traveled to Bartlesville, Oklahoma to work on a project. I shouldn't have been surprised to find that Bartlesville was smack dab in the heart of oil country. I also learned that finding healthy options for restaurant meals was as difficult as fishing for a half-eaten dog treat under the sofa.

Server: "May I take your order, sir?"

Me: "Hi. You've got lots of options on your menu; what do you recommend?"

Server: "The chicken-fried steak is popular. It's a 14-ounce steak with green-bean/bacon casserole, mashed potatoes, gravy, and complimentary apple pie à la mode."

Me: "That's a little heavy for me. Anything more on the lighter side?"

Server (now pursing her lips and squinting at me): "We serve a lot of ribeye steak platters, with fried mushrooms and gravy, and twice-fried steak fries."

Me (closing the menu): "You know, maybe I'll just have the salad bar."

Server: "Sir, we don't have a salad bar. I think the Wendy's off I-60 by the truck depot might have a salad bar. Or, I can bring you a side salad with iceberg lettuce, French dressing, and one tomato. Those are your options."

Me (unfolding my white dinner napkin in defeat): "I'll have the side salad please."

Duly noted

Reg's sticky note habit was well observed, and the notoriety of his addiction well deserved. At any time of day, an office visitor might find sticky notes perched between the keys on his computer keyboard like a mezzanine full of concertgoers. But they also graced his monitor, writing tablets, and mobile phone and were sometimes stuck on his car keys sitting on his desk.

The written messages covered myriad topics and included such mundane phrases as:

> Gas at lunch
> Budget Mtg @ 1:00
> Call contractor Thurs — kitch remodel
> Interview C.C. Baxter
> Change oil wkend

While the eccentricity of his note taking was a puzzlement, staff pretty much agreed he was never late for appointments, was always prepared for meetings, and managed his time wisely.

At home, the sticky note habit was also in full force, although these notes were all of a domestic nature. His wife found them amusing and occasionally so cryptic that they required some explanation.

One day, Reg drove to the lot where his wife typically parked at her work and slipped a note under her windshield wiper blade.

That afternoon, a parking attendant noticed that Reg's wife's car was over the paid-for time limit, and she looked at the note stuck under the wiper blade. It read:

> Wash the car
> Pick up milk on the way home
> Tell your sweetie that you love her   ♡

The parking attendant smiled at the romantic gesture and said, "aw. . . " to herself. She then carefully replaced the note, filled out a parking ticket, and placed it under the other wiper blade.

Visualizing time

I'm fascinated by the way people visualize the days of the week. Having canvassed a few friends at work, I learned that some see the days as they are arranged on the calendar (the week ends on Saturday and begins on Sunday). Others picture the calendar days in a single horizontal sequence of numbered dates.

In my mind, I imagine the days of the week in the form of a racetrack, which kind of makes sense when you think about how much we endeavor to speed through the week to get to the weekend.

In my model, I visualize the five weekdays on one leg of the track, and the weekend on the other leg. Notably, Saturday and Sunday are longer because they generally convey fun and leisurely activity.

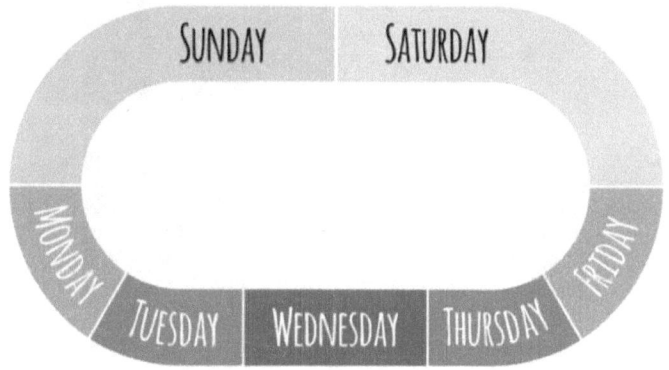

Definitions

multitasking, noun

mul·ti·task·ing (multē′tasking)

Doing four or five tasks at the same time—poorly.

infinity, noun

in·fin·i·ty (in′finitē)

The number of times it takes to sweep the last bit of dust into the dustbin.

Rental cars

Neither Sherri nor I were experts on the makes and models of automobiles. This deficit was magnified by our perception of car colors. What I thought was silvery green was jasmine to her. What she thought was deep maroon was burgundy red to me.

Ordinarily, this wouldn't be a problem, except that the two of us were in Pennsylvania working on a high-stress proposal, and we kept forgetting where we parked our rental car.

In 2004, Toyotas looked like Hondas; some Nissans looked like Mazdas; GM and Ford sedans looked very much alike. Because we didn't have a key fob to honk our car's horn or flash our lights, we relied on our color perceptions to locate the bloomin' thing.

Consequently, Sherri and I were late to practically every meeting and lunch engagement on our tour of duty.

We never could find that car . . .

TECHNOLOGY

Anchors aweigh

I think the twin sunshades I got for my Forester are too big. When not in use, they're the kind you twist and turn to collapse into ovals, then secure with an elastic band.

So, my wife and I return from some outing. I reach around the seat to retrieve the sunshades, slip the elastic band off, give the thing a twist, and the shades spring open with the intensity of someone pulling the inflation cord on a rubber dinghy, pinning both of us to our seats.

I see a trip to auto parts store in the near future.

My first smartphone

I'll never forget the day I purchased my first smartphone. The event was on par with getting my learner's permit, passing my SAT, or going on my first date. I was, in fact, bracing myself to navigate this corner on the information highway.

The salesperson patiently explained all the features of my new, out-of-the-box pocket computer (a.k.a. smartphone). She walked me through icons, apps, and settings on the device, occasionally looking up to see if I was getting it. Judging from her expression, I gathered that I looked as if she were explaining Einstein's theory of general relativity.

(I'm generally good at picking up new technology tools, but the smartphone seemed to have endless layers of obscure settings that needed to be set for optimal performance.)

The salesperson then showed me how to use my opposable thumbs (boy, aren't those handy?) to compose and send a text.

When I left the store, I felt somehow smarter and more worldly, and thought that maybe I should accent my wardrobe with some new clothes to reflect this new confidence. I slipped the smartphone into my jeans pocket and off I went.

THE NEIGHBORHOOD

Walkabout

See them strolling through the neighborhood. There's the old fellow ambling along and reading what looks like a hardbound textbook. He never looks up and never trips over curbs, driveways, or cracks in the sidewalks.

Then there's the young professional taking a brisk walk on his lunch break and eating his salad while he goes. We think he's the veterinarian who works nearby.

Look to the right and you'll see the gal on her smartphone walking four greyhounds, each one twice her size. But without so much as a slip or stumble, they navigate the craggy sidewalk as though it were a memorized obstacle course.

The Good Samaritan breaking bad

In my younger days, my Dad began to experience lower back pain, likely exacerbated by working in a lumber yard in his teens and, much later, maintaining the family automobiles. His lower back aches tended to come and go, but I recall one of his worst bouts occurring one mid-summer weekend when he was laid out in his easy chair.

Enter our next-door neighbor, Jack Wettlaufer, who was a dead ringer for Dennis the Menace's Dad in the funnies. He was a kindly fellow who would go out of his way to help the neighbors, particularly if someone was sick or out of town. But Jack was also accident prone and often left disasters in his wake—albeit while performing good deeds like raking and bagging up your leaves or shoveling your sidewalk after a hearty snow.

It was my Dad who answered the phone by his recliner. "Jay, I hear you're laid low with some back trouble. How's about me mowing your front yard for ya?" I could tell my Dad was barely able to process the information, let alone think of a polite way to decline the offer. "Sure, sure Jack. Whatever."

Moments after the lawnmower started up, a KER-THUNK! sound shot through the house like a jet breaking the sound barrier. My Dad and I looked at each other as we heard Jack shout from the front yard, "Oh for heaven's sake, I've gone and clipped a sprinkler head. Oh goodness gracious!"

Dad looked at me for moment, closed his eyes, then flopped back down in the chair. It would only be a matter of time before the Good Samaritan would strike again. But we held the distinction of being the first in a string of incidents that would keep the neighborhood in turmoil for years to come.

Plants of the Southwest

The famed Mickey Mouse Cactus.

WORDS

Listen

On a Zoom call this week with friends, we touched upon the importance of being a good listener. I was reminded of reading Harpo Marx's wonderful biography, *Harpo Speaks!*, where I learned that one of the virtues of the comic actor's career-spanning, on-screen silence was that he was a devout listener. Harpo was welcomed into every stratum of society, but he was particularly popular with intellectuals, theater critics, and writers in New York. He was admired because he listened in order to learn, and only spoke when he had something relevant to say.

Speak English please

My high school friend's mother, whom we addressed as Mrs. Henderson, was a public school English teacher in the '60s and '70s. I remember the time four of us buddies gathered in the entryway of my friend's house, jacketing up to go have a snowball fight.

As Mrs. Henderson stepped around us in the entryway, she said, "What's up?"

Kenny explained, "We're just conjugating in the hall."

She stopped in her tracks and looked over at Kenny. "Conjugating?"

We knew Kenny meant to say congregating, but to recover, I quickly pitched this explanation:

"You know, Mrs. Henderson, I throw, you throw, he throws, we throw snowballs."

Mrs. Henderson shook her head and said, "You teenagers are so weird."

The thing is . . .

Some language shortcuts just work. Though it's been drilled into me to be precise in my writing and speaking, I've often found that the simplest workaround prevails. Take the nebulous noun, "thing."

Two groups of friends: "We'll meet you at the thing, under the canopy by the thing." (It's as reliable as GPS.)

Recalling a favorite meal: "We had eggplant parmesan, a side of pasta, and some thing (not something) with mushrooms and artichoke hearts."

Someone closes their argument with a simple summation: "The thing is, it's the right thing to do."

A music listener yells out, "Play that thing!" to a bluegrass banjo picker.

A student who can't quite recall the four crops harvested by a bygone civilization writes: "The Aztecs grew maize, beans, and . . . other things."

A person expressing righteous indignation: "The thing that really irks me is . . . "

I submit that "thing" is a useful . . . well, thing.

First lines in works of fiction

In 1897, Stephen Crane wrote a short story titled, "The Open Boat," about four sailors who are set adrift in a dinghy after a shipwreck.

The story opens with what I believe is one of the most beautiful first lines in American fiction:

"None of them knew the color of the sky."

In the simplest terms, none of sailors know their fate. Will they be rescued; will they be capsized and drowned by an indifferent universe; or will Providence intervene and return them safely to the shore?

Coffee house culture

While reading and slurping up a frothy cappuccino at a cafe, I kept peeking over the top of my book to observe a table of four attempting to solve the New York Times daily crossword puzzle. I recognized two of the fellows as local theatre actors, not by name, but by their wildly animated expressions and broad gestures. I knew I'd seen one in a modernized version of Hamlet.

As the collaboration charged on, one fellow, digging deeply in his memory, jumped up from his chair several times and circled the table, only to flop down again in frustration. Finally, the Hamlet actor leaned across the table and pressed his finger on the puzzle.

"It's not a park in Montgomery . . . it's Rosa Parks!"

An unexpected change of heart

Have you ever found yourself in a spirited disagreement with a friend when—at the zenith of your Platonic logic and Shakespearean eloquence—you suddenly see the merit of their argument and reasoning? You may find it hard to recover without stammering, as you feel the balloon of your opinion deflating rapidly.

The best return I can generally come up with is, "Wow . . . I never thought of that."

WHAT IF?

Days of the pandemic

Wyatt Earp sits on the portico in front of the hotel, leaning back in his chair. His brother comes up to chat.

Virgil: "Waitin' on the Clanton boys, Wyatt?"

Wyatt Earp: "Nope. I reckon the Fed Ex stage should be gettin' in right about now."

Virgil: "Order somethin'?"

Wyatt Earp: "Nope. Just kinda gotten used to seein' 'em come through town."

Modern antiquities

They're building a mammoth Amazon Fulfillment Center at the top of the west mesa in Albuquerque, just south of the volcanoes. My wife and I took a trip to see it up close, and it is BIG!

How big, you ask?

It's so big that 2,000 years from now archaeologists will unearth it and determine that it was built in honor of our emperors or kings and that the strange conveyors inside were in fact passageways into the crypt. There, they'll surely discover thousands of ancient artifacts like iPads, kitchen utensils, exercise equipment, clothing, and more.

IT GAVE ME PAUSE

The ER

Home at 1:00 a.m. Mom and I spent six hours together in the emergency room of Presbyterian Hospital last night. Her assisted living home had contacted me earlier that day with concerns that she might have a UTI. This is a ritual we've been through many times; before my mom, with my brother, and before him, my dad. Fortunately, mom slept pretty deeply the whole time, for which I was thankful.

No point in describing the ER in the middle of the night. It must be pretty much the same everywhere in America. It's where most of our poorest and most marginalized citizens receive medical care.

I wasn't surprised to see several homeless people in the waiting area. But there was also a family of four that seemed in the middle of a crisis I couldn't ascertain. At first, it was just the mother and her two boys. I would make them out to be between four and seven, and they were squirming and making noise as children will do at 11:00 at night.

After a time, the father came stomping through the swinging outside doors and flung his jacket on a chair, part of which landed on one of the boys. The couple then engaged in a hushed conversation, with the man clearly agitated. Something wasn't right. All I could gather was something about a missed phone call, a wrong number, and a scheduled meeting that never took place.

The boys kept asking their father when they were going to go and when Grandma was going to get them.

The man turned from his wife and shouted at them to "Shut up! I just want you to sit there and SHUT THE F**K UP!"

But the boys kept on and the younger of the two rolled a toy tank up his father's calf, talking in a sing-song voice. The man spun around and, physically wrenching the toy out of his hand, threw it across the waiting room.

For a fleeting moment, several of us in the waiting room stood up without knowing exactly what we should do. We looked for the security guard who had been through maybe ten minutes earlier.

This time leaning into his son's face, almost touching his nose, he yelled louder still, "I told you to SIT DOWN and SHUT UP!"

Then, the homeless woman left her companion and stepped lightly over to the father, careful not to invade his space.

In the mildest voice imaginable she said, "Mister, you shouldn't yell at your kids like that—"

"Why don't you mind your own business, b*tch!"

She paused, looking down, then, meeting his eyes said, "—unless you want them to turn out like me."

The lady next door

For years, my wife and I lived next door to a widowed woman who lived into her late nineties. We would look in on her and help her out if she needed some simple things done, like changing batteries in her radio, oiling the hinges on her front door, getting her a gallon of milk. One thing we realized after years of being neighbors is that, in her isolation, her only points of reference to the world were television news, a radio, and the daily newspaper. It always made us sad to see how bitter she had become over the years, but we would listen patiently to her describe how the world had become a wicked, frightening place.

We learned something valuable about the dangers of having a narrow field of view of the world around you.

He was a quiet young man

He woke up when his mind and body no longer needed rest. He collected his clothes scattered across the bedroom carpet, dressed, looked at himself in the bathroom mirror, then stepped into the kitchen to gather his keys and wallet and pocket change from the counter. He checked the refrigerator one last time to ensure there were no perishable items left there. Everything else in the house was left as is: the bed and bedding, the furniture, the curtains, the lamps, the framed pictures.

Taking his coat from the closet off the entryway into the house, he folded it under his arm and opened the front door. Without looking back, he stepped onto the porch, locked the house, and drove 1,600 miles to live with his parents.

That's how the house was left five years ago and how it remains to this day—except for plywood panels boarding up the windows and doors. Its future is caught up in the courts and still unresolved.

Rite of passage

When I was five or six my favorite uncle died on a farm in Indiana. My brother and I were told that he was out walking with his hunting dog, Henry-boy, sat down in the shade of a cottonwood tree, and had a massive heart attack.

My mother's younger brother, Roy, was just 33 years old at the time of his death. He'd been in the Service—the Army, I think—had spent some time in Bangkok—where he'd gotten married to a very young Asian woman—had been a motorcycle cop for the Des Moines Police Department, and had then returned home to my grandparent's house, where he lived from time to time.

The thing I remember most about this time is that for months after Roy's death, everyone whispered and talked behind closed doors, took private phone calls, always watching me and my brother closely as if they were waiting for us to ask difficult questions. We never did.

A year or two later, as I sat with a drawing pad on the window-niche bed in my grandparent's house, my grandmother talked casually about death while I copied drawings out of my uncle's sketch book. I practiced forming the loose geometric shapes that would eventually become a cartoon rabbit's head, a rotund belly, and a bushy tail, and my grandmother explained that all people living today would one day die, just as Roy had. She smiled that great Walter Brennan smile of hers when she said it, as if this was something wonderous like a rainbow or a bed of roses.

I spent the afternoon playing around the wood piles behind the house and sitting in the vacant lot to the north of their property sifting sand through my clenched hand into the palm of the other. I pondered what she had said and, for the first time, understood that everything has an end, including me.

ABOUT THE AUTHOR

Kevin Hughes is a life-long native of Albuquerque, New Mexico, where he lives with his wife, Mary. Earning his bachelor's degree in English in 1979, he has been a professional musician, composer and songwriter, technical writer, instructional designer, and video producer and director. As a writer, Kevin favors the short story form, which can reveal truths through life-changing events occurring within a brief moment in time. Inspired by the works of O. Henry, Shirley Jackson, John Updike, and Anthony Doerr, Kevin has presented four short stories in this collection, followed by "shorter stories" that are mostly humorous, non-fiction anecdotes and musings.